Jack London

the CALL of the WILD

adapted by

Charles Dixon and Ricardo Villagran
script   artist

lettered by Gary Fields

CLASSICS ILLUSTRATED

BERKLEY/ FIRST PUBLISHING

As many authors have done, Jack London used his own experiences to enrich his writing. But while other writers simply have called upon their pasts to produce fiction assembled from thinly veiled autobiography, London fashioned his unique stories from the knowledge he gained during an adventure-filled life. London's most popular works, his short stories and novels of the Yukon, resulted from his travels and encounters during an ill-fated attempt in 1897 to glean a fortune in the Klondike gold rush. These pieces are remarkable not only for their narrative power, but for their insights into the social behavior of men and animals. The first of London's Yukon stories began appearing in magazines in 1898; his first collection, *The Son of the Wolf,* was published in 1900. In quick succession, London's major novels of the Yukon appeared: **The Call of the Wild** (1903), *White Fang* (1906), *Burning Daylight* (1910), and *Smoke Bellew* (1912). Tiring of the Victorian staleness that continued to pervade most American fiction through the beginning of the twentieth century, readers revelled in London's raw, often bloody, celebrations of the rapidly vanishing frontier. The novels quickly won popular acclaim for their spirit of adventure, courage, and individual struggle, and garnered critical renown for their perceptive portraits of the vigorous yet brutal character of nature. Today, London is still recognized for his ability to craft stunning fiction that incorporated a variety of challenging philosophical concepts. Like many of London's novels, **The Call of the Wild** is a fascinating weave. It is a spellbinding animal story, perhaps the best ever written; it is an excellent dramatization of the laws of nature; and it is an illuminating study of the beastly manners of civilized men and the civilized manners of beasts.

The Call of the Wild
Classics Illustrated, Number 10

Wade Roberts, Editorial Director
Alex Wald, Art Director
Mike McCormick, Production Manager

PRINTING HISTORY
1st edition published June 1990

For information, address: First Publishing, Inc., 435 North LaSalle St., Chicago, Illinois 60610.

ISBN 0-425-12030-9

Distributed by Berkley Sales & Marketing, a division of The Berkley Publishing Group, 200 Madison Avenue, New York, New York 10016.

Printed in the United States of America
1 2 3 4 5 6 7 8 9 0

BUCK DID NOT READ THE NEWS-PAPERS, OR HE WOULD HAVE KNOWN THAT TROUBLE WAS BREWING. NOT ALONE FOR HIMSELF, BUT FOR EVERY TIDEWATER DOG FROM PUGET SOUND TO SAN DIEGO.

BECAUSE MEN, GROPING IN THE ARTIC DARKNESS, HAD FOUND A YELLOW METAL.

THESE MEN WANTED DOGS WITH STRONG MUSCLES BY WHICH TO TOIL, AND FURRY COATS TO PROTECT THEM FROM THE FROST.

BUCK LIVED AT A BIG HOUSE IN THE SUN-KISSED SANTA CLARA VALLEY. JUDGE MILLER'S PLACE, IT WAS CALLED.

IT STOOD BACK FROM THE ROAD, HALF HIDDEN FROM THE TREES.

THERE WERE GREAT STABLES, ROWS OF VINE-CLAD SER-VANTS' COTTAGES, AN ORDERLY ARRAY OF OUTHOUSES, GRAPE ARBORS, GREEN PAS-TURES, ORCHARDS AND BERRY PATCHES.

AND OVER THIS GREAT DEMESNE BUCK RULED.

HERE HE WAS BORN, AND HERE HE LIVED THE FOUR YEARS OF HIS LIFE. IT WAS TRUE THERE WERE OTHER DOGS ON THE PLACE, BUT THEY DID NOT COUNT.

HE WAS KING--KING OVER ALL CREEPING, CRAWLING, FLYING THINGS OF JUDGE MILLER'S PLACE.

BUCK WAS NEITHER HOUSE DOG NOR KENNEL DOG. THE WHOLE REALM WAS HIS.

HUMANS INCLUDED.

AND THIS WAS THE MANNER OF DOG BUCK WAS IN THE FALL OF 1897, WHEN THE KLONDIKE STRIKE DRAGGED MEN FROM ALL THE WORLD INTO THE FROZEN NORTH.

MANUEL, ONE OF THE GARDENER'S HELPERS, HAD ONE BESETTING SIN. HE LOVED TO PLAY CHINESE LOTTERY. HE HAD FAITH IN A SYSTEM, AND THIS MADE HIS DAMNATION CERTAIN.

FOR TO PLAY A SYSTEM REQUIRES MONEY...

...WHILE THE WAGES OF A GARDENER'S HELPER DO NOT LAP OVER THE NEEDS OF A WIFE AND NUMEROUS PROGENY.

THE JUDGE WAS AT A MEETING OF THE RAISIN GROWERS ASSOCIATION, AND THE BOYS WERE BUSY ORGANIZING AN ATHLETIC CLUB ON THE NIGHT OF MANUEL'S TREACHERY.

NO ONE SAW HIM AND BUCK GO OFF THROUGH THE ORCHARD ON WHAT BUCK IMAGINED WAS MERELY A STROLL.

NO ONE SAW THEM ARRIVE AT A LITTLE FLAG STATION KNOWN AS COLLEGE PARK.

WHEN THE ENDS OF THE ROPE WERE PLACED IN THE STRANGER'S HANDS, BUCK GROWLED MENACINGLY.

BUT, TO HIS SURPRISE, THE ROPE TIGHTENED AROUND HIS NECK, SHUTTING OFF HIS BREATH.

THEN THE ROPE TIGHTENED MERCILESSLY, WHILE BUCK STRUGGLED IN A FURY.

NEVER IN HIS LIFE HAD HE BEEN SO VILELY TREATED, AND NEVER HAD HE BEEN SO ANGRY.

BUT HIS STRENGTH EBBED, AND HIS EYES GLAZED...

THE NEXT THING HE KNEW, HE WAS BEING JOLTED ALONG IN SOME SORT OF CONVEYANCE. THE HOARSE SHRIEK OF A LOCOMOTIVE TOLD HIM WHERE HE WAS.

T HERE HE LAY, NURSING HIS WRATH AND WOUNDED PRIDE.

FOR TWO DAYS AND NIGHTS THIS EXPRESS CAR WAS DRAGGED ALONG AT THE TAIL OF SHRIEK-ING LOCOMOTIVES.

AND FOR TWO DAYS AND NIGHTS BUCK NEITHER ATE NOR DRANK.

HE COULD NOT UNDERSTAND WHAT IT ALL MEANT. WHAT DID THEY WANT WITH HIM, THESE STRANGE MEN?

HIS EYES TURNED BLOOD-SHOT, AND HE WAS METAMORPHOSED INTO A RAGING FIEND. SO CHANGED WAS HE THAT THE JUDGE HIMSELF WOULD NOT HAVE RECOGNIZED HIM.

THE EXPRESS MANAGERS BREATHED WITH RELIEF WHEN THEY BUNDLED HIM OFF THE TRAIN IN SEATTLE.

A STOUT MAN CAME OUT AND SIGNED THE BOOK FOR THE DRIVER. THAT WAS THE MAN, BUCK DIVINED, THE NEXT TORMENTOR.

HAIR BRISTLING, MOUTH FOAMING, A MAD GLITTER IN HIS EYES, HE LAUNCHED HIS ONE HUNDRED AND FORTY POUNDS OF FURY AT THE MAN.

H E WAS BEATEN; BUT HE WAS NOT BROKEN.

THE CLUB WAS A REVELATION. IT WAS HIS INTRODUCTION TO THE REIGN OF PRIMITIVE LAW, AND HE MET THE INTRODUCTION HALFWAY.

THE FACTS OF LIFE TOOK ON A FIERCER ASPECT; AND WHILE HE FACED THAT ASPECT UNCOWED, HE FACED IT WITH ALL THE LATENT CUNNING OF HIS NATURE AROUSED.

NOW AND AGAIN MEN CAME WHO TALKED EXCITEDLY, WHEEDLING, AND IN ALL KINDS OF FASHIONS TO THE MAN IN THE RED SWEATER.

AND AT SUCH TIMES THAT MONEY PASSED BETWEEN THEM THE STRANGERS TOOK ONE OR MORE OF THE DOGS AWAY WITH THEM.

BUCK'S TIME CAME IN THE FORM OF A LITTLE WEAZENED MAN WHO SPAT BROKEN ENGLISH.

SACREDAM! DAT ONE FINE BULLY DOG! HOW MOCH?

THREE HUNDRED AND A PRESENT AT THAT!

BUCK SAW MONEY PASS BETWEEN THEM, AND WAS NOT SURPRISED WHEN CURLY, A GOOD-NATURED NEWFOUNDLAND, AND HE WERE LED AWAY BY THE LITTLE MAN.

THAT WAS THE LAST BUCK SAW OF THE MAN IN THE RED SWEATER.

AND AS CURLY AND HE LOOKED AT RECEDING SEATTLE FROM THE DECK OF THE NARWHAL, IT WAS THE LAST HE SAW OF THE WARM SOUTHLAND.

DAY AND NIGHT THE SHIP THROBBED TO THE TIRELESS PULSE OF THE PROPELLER, THOUGH ONE DAY WAS LIKE ANOTHER, IT WAS APPARENT TO BUCK THAT THE WEATHER WAS STEADILY GROWING COLDER.

AT LAST, ONE MORNING, THE PROPELLER WAS QUIET AND THE NARWHAL WAS PERVADED WITH AN ATMOSPHERE OF EXCITEMENT.

AT FIRST STEP INTO THE WHITE MUSH, HE SPRANG BACK WITH A SNORT. HE SHOOK HIMSELF, BUT MORE OF IT FELL UPON HIM. THE ONLOOKERS LAUGHED UPROARIOUSLY, AND HE FELT ASHAMED.

HE KNEW NOT WHY, FOR IT WAS HIS FIRST SNOW.

BUCK'S FIRST DAY ON THE DYEA BEACH WAS LIKE A NIGHTMARE. EVERY HOUR WAS FILLED WITH SHOCK AND SURPRISE. HERE WAS NEITHER PEACE, NOR REST, NOR A MOMENT'S SAFETY.

THESE WERE NOT TOWN DOGS AND MEN. THEY WERE SAVAGES, ALL OF THEM, WHO KNEW NO LAW BUT THE LAW OF CLUB AND FANG.

HE HAD NEVER SEEN DOGS FIGHT AS THESE WOLFISH CREATURES FOUGHT. IT WAS THE WOLF MANNER OF FIGHTING, TO STRIKE AND LEAP AWAY.

CURLY WAS THE VICTIM.

SO THAT WAS THE WAY. NO FAIR PLAY. ONCE DOWN, THAT WAS THE END OF YOU.

A WHITE SPITZBERGEN RAN OUT HIS TONGUE AND LAUGHED AGAIN, AND FROM THAT MOMENT BUCK HATED HIM WITH A BITTER AND DEATH-LESS HATRED.

AS HE HAD SEEN HORSES WORK, SO BUCK WAS SET TO WORK. THE HALF-BREED FRANÇOIS FASTENED UPON HIM AN ARRANGEMENT OF STRAPS AND BUCKLES.

THOUGH HIS DIGNITY WAS SORELY HURT, HE WAS TOO WISE TO REBEL.

THE NEXT MORNING, THEY WERE SWINGING UP TOWARD THE DYEA CAÑON. IT WAS A HARD RUN, UP THE CAÑON, THROUGH SHEEP CAMP, PAST SCALES AND THE TIMBERLINE...

...AND OVER THE GREAT CHILKOOT DIVIDE, WHICH GUARDS FORBIDDINGLY THE SAD AND LONELY NORTH.

DAY AFTER DAY, FOR DAYS UNENDING, BUCK TOILED IN THE TRACES. ALWAYS, THEY BROKE CAMP IN THE DARK AND THE FIRST GRAY OF DAWN FOUND THEM HITTING THE TRAIL.

AND ALWAYS THEY PITCHED CAMP AFTER DARK, EATING THEIR BIT OF FISH, AND CRAWLING TO SLEEP IN THE SNOW.

BUCK NEVER HAD ENOUGH.

SO GREATLY DID HUNGER COMPEL HIM, HE WAS NOT ABOVE TAKING WHAT DID NOT BELONG TO HIM.

THIS FIRST THEFT MARKED BUCK AS FIT TO SURVIVE IN THE HOSTILE ENVIRONMENT.

HE DID NOT STEAL FOR JOY OF IT; BUT BECAUSE OF THE CLAMOR OF HIS STOMACH.

HE DID NOT ROB OPENLY, BUT STOLE SECRETLY AND CUNNINGLY, OUT OF RESPECT FOR CLUB AND FANG.

INSTINCTS LONG DEAD BECAME ALIVE AGAIN.

HE REMEMBERED BACK TO THE YOUTH OF THE BREED, TO THE TIME WILD DOGS RANGED IN PACKS THROUGH THE FOREST AND KILLED THEIR MEAT AS THEY RAN IT DOWN.

AND WHEN, ON THE STILL COLD NIGHTS, HE POINTED AND HOWLED LONG AND WOLF-LIKE, IT WAS HIS ANCESTORS, DEAD AND DUST, POINTING AND HOWLING DOWN THROUGH THE CENTURIES AND THROUGH HIM.

HIS CADENCES WERE THEIR CADENCES, VOICING THEIR WOE AND WHAT TO THEM WAS THE MEANING OF THE STILLNESS, AND THE COLD, AND DARK.

ONE MORNING, PIKE, A MALINGERER, DID NOT APPEAR. FRAN-ÇOIS CALLED AND SOUGHT HIM IN VAIN.

SPITZ WAS WILD WITH WRATH. HE RAGED THROUGH THE CAMP, SMELLING AND DIGGING IN EVERY LIKELY PLACE, SNARLING FRIGHT-FULLY.

WHEN PIKE WAS AT LAST UNEARTHED, SPITZ FLEW AT HIM TO PUNISH HIM.

AND SUDDENLY, BUCK FLEW, WITH EQUAL RAGE, IN BETWEEN.

PIKE TOOK HEART AT THIS OPEN MUTINY, AND SPRANG UPON HIS OVERTHROWN LEADER.

BUT FRANÇOIS, UNSWERVING IN THE ADMINISTRATION OF JUSTICE, BROUGHT HIS LASH DOWN UPON BUCK WITH ALL HIS MIGHT.

BUCK, TO WHOM FAIR-PLAY WAS A FORGOTTEN CODE, LIKEWISE SPRANG UPON SPITZ.

THE LASH WAS LAID UPON HIM AGAIN AND AGAIN, WHILE SPITZ SOUNDLY PUNISHED THE MANY-TIMES OFFENDING PIKE.

IN THE DAYS THAT FOLLOWED, BUCK STILL CONTINUED TO INTERFERE BETWEEN SPITZ AND THE CULPRITS... BUT HE DID IT CRAFTILY.

WITH THE COVERT MUTINY OF BUCK, A GENERAL INSUBORDINATION SPRANG UP AND INCREASED. THINGS NO LONGER WENT RIGHT, AND THERE WAS CONTINUAL BICKERING.

TROUBLE WAS ALWAYS AFOOT, AND AT THE BOTTOM OF IT WAS BUCK.

HE KEPT FRANÇOIS BUSY, FOR THE DOG-DRIVER WAS IN CONSTANT APPREHENSION OF THE LIFE-AND-DEATH STRUGGLE HE KNEW MUST TAKE PLACE SOONER OR LATER.

BUT THE OPPORTUNITY DID NOT PRESENT ITSELF.

HERE THERE WERE MANY MEN, AND COUNTLESS DOGS.

EVERY NIGHT, THEY LIFTED A NOCTURNAL SONG, A WEIRD AND EERIE CHANT, IN WHICH IT WAS BUCK'S DELIGHT TO JOIN.

IT WAS AN OLD SONG-- ONE OF THE FIRST SONGS OF THE YOUNGER WORLD IN A DAY WHEN SONGS WERE SAD.

SEVEN DAYS FROM THE TIME THEY PULLED INTO DAWSON, THEY DROPPED DOWN A STEEP BANK TO THE YUKON TRAIL AND PULLED FOR DYEA AND SALT WATER.

THE INSIDIOUS REVOLT LED BY BUCK HAD DESTROYED THE SOLIDARITY OF THE TEAM.

NO MORE WAS SPITZ A LEADER TO BE FEARED. THE OLD AWE DEPARTED, AND THEY GREW EQUAL TO CHALLENGING HIS AUTHORITY.

BUCK'S CONDUCT APPROACHED THAT OF A BULLY, AND HE WAS GIVEN TO SWAGGERING UP AND DOWN BEFORE SPITZ'S VERY NOSE.

AT THE MOUTH OF THE TAHKEENA, ONE NIGHT AFTER SUPPER, DUB TURNED UP A SNOW-SHOE RABBIT, BLUNDERED IT, AND MISSED.

IN A SECOND THE WHOLE TEAM WAS IN FULL CRY. A HUNDRED YARDS AWAY WAS A CAMP OF THE NORTH-WEST POLICE WITH FIFTY DOGS WHO JOINED THE CHASE.

EVERY ANIMAL WAS MOTIONLESS AS THOUGH TURNED TO STONE.

ONLY SPITZ QUIVERED AND BRISTLED AS HE STAGGERED, SNARLING WITH HORRIBLE MENACE, AS THOUGH TO FRIGHTEN OFF IMPENDING DEATH.

THE DARK CIRCLE CLOSED ON THE MOON-FLOODED SNOW AS SPITZ DISAPPEARED FROM VIEW.

BUCK STOOD AND LOOKED ON, THE SUCCESSFUL CHAMPION...

...THE DOMINANT PRIMORDIAL BEAST WHO HAD MADE HIS KILL AND FOUND IT GOOD.

EH? WOT I SAY? I SPIK TRUE W'EN I SAY DAT BUCK TWO DEVILS.

DAT SPITZ FIGHT LAK HELL.

BUCK TROTTED UP TO THE PLACE SPITZ WOULD HAVE OCCUPIED AS LEADER; BUT FRANÇOIS BROUGHT SOL-LEKS TO THE COVETED POSITION.

NOW WE MAKE GOOD TIME. NO MORE SPITZ, NO MORE TROUBLE, SURE.

BUCK SPRANG UPON SOL-LEKS IN A FURY, DRIVING HIM BACK AND STANDING IN HIS PLACE.

EH? LOOK AT DAT BUCK. HEEM KEEL DAT SPITZ, HEEM T'INK TO TAKE DE JOB.

PERRAULT TOOK A HAND. BETWEEN THEM THEY RAN BUCK ABOUT FOR THE BETTER PART OF AN HOUR. THEY CURSED HIM AND HIS FATHERS AND MOTHERS BEFORE HIM.

GO 'WAY, CHOOK!

HE ANSWERED EVERY CURSE WITH A SNARL AND KEPT OUT OF THEIR REACH, ADVERTISING PLAINLY THAT WHEN HIS DESIRE WAS MET, HE WOULD COME IN AND BE GOOD.

TIME WAS FLYING, AND THEY SHOULD HAVE BEEN ON THE TRAIL AN HOUR GONE.

FRANÇOIS SHRUGGED HIS SHOULDERS IN A SIGN THAT THEY WERE BEATEN.

T'ROW DOWN DE CLUB.

BUCK TROTTED IN, LAUGHING TRIUMPHANTLY, AND SWUNG AROUND INTO POSITION AT THE HEAD OF THE TEAM.

BUCK'S TRACES WERE FASTENED, THE SLED BROKEN OUT, AND WITH BOTH MEN RUNNING THEY DASHED OUT ON THE RIVER TRAIL.

HIGHLY AS FRANÇOIS HAD FORE-VALUED BUCK, HE FOUND, WHILE THE DAY WAS YET YOUNG, THAT HE HAD UNDERVALUED.

AT A BOUND BUCK TOOK UP THE DUTIES OF LEADERSHIP, HE SHOWED HIMSELF THE SUPERIOR OF EVEN SPITZ, OF WHOM FRANÇOIS HAD NEVER SEEN AN EQUAL.

THE TEAM RECOVERED ITS OLD-TIME SOLIDARITY, AND ONCE MORE THE DOGS LEAPED AS ONE DOG IN THE TRACES.

THEY COVERED THE THIRTY MILE RIVER IN ONE DAY GOING OUT WHAT HAD TAKEN THEM TEN DAYS COMING IN.

ON THE LAST NIGHT OF THE SECOND WEEK THEY TOPPED WHITE PASS AND DROPPED DOWN THE SEA SLOPE WITH THE LIGHTS OF SKAGWAY AT THEIR FEET.

IN ONE RUN THEY MADE A SIXTY-MILE DASH FROM THE FOOT OF LAKE LEBARGE TO THE WHITE HORSE RAPIDS.

I T WAS A RECORD RUN.

FOR THREE DAYS PERRAULT AND FRANCOIS THREW CHESTS UP AND DOWN THE MAIN STREET OF SKAGWAY AND WERE DELUGED WITH INVITATIONS TO DRINK.

NEXT CAME OFFICIAL ORDERS. LIKE OTHER MEN, PERRAULT AND FRANCOIS PASSED OUT OF BUCK'S LIFE FOREVER.

A SCOTCH HALF-BREED TOOK CHARGE OF HIM AND HIS MATES, AND IN COMPANY WITH A DOZEN OTHER DOG TEAMS HE STARTED...

...BACK OVER THE WEARY TRAIL TO DAWSON. IT WAS NO LIGHT RUNNING NOW, NOR RECORD TIME, BUT HEAVY TOIL EACH DAY.

THIS WAS THE MAIL TRAIN, CARRYING WORD FROM THE WORLD TO MEN WHO SOUGHT GOLD UNDER THE SHADOW OF THE POLE.

IT WAS MORE THAN TWO MONTHS BEFORE THE SALT WATER MAIL, WITH A PROUD BUCK AT THE FORE, ARRIVED BACK AT SKAG-WAY.

THE DOGS WERE IN A WRETCHED STATE, WORN OUT AND WORN DOWN.

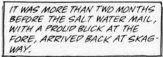

HAL'S WHIP FELL UPON THE DOGS. THEY THREW THEMSELVES AGAINST THE BREASTBANDS, AND PUT FORTH ALL THEIR STRENGTH. THE SLED HELD AS THOUGH IT WERE AN ANCHOR.

AFTER TWO EFFORTS, THEY STOOD STILL, PANTING. THE WHIP WAS WHISTLING SAVAGELY, WHEN MERCEDES INTERFERED.

YOU POOR, POOR DEARS. WHY DON'T YOU PULL HARD? -- THEN YOU WON'T BE WHIPPED.

IT'S NOT THAT I CARE A WHOOP WHAT BECOMES OF YOU--

BUT YOU CAN HELP THEM DOGS A MIGHTY LOT BY BREAKING OUT THAT SLED.

THE RUNNERS ARE FROZE FAST. THROW YOUR WEIGHT AGAINST THE GEE-POLE, AND BREAK IT OUT.

A THIRD TIME THE ATTEMPT WAS MADE, AND THE OVERLOADED AND UNWIELDY SLED FINALLY FORGED AHEAD.

B UCK AND HIS MATES STRUGGLED FRANTIC-ALLY UNDER THE RAIN OF BLOWS.

A HUNDRED YARDS AHEAD THE PATH TURNED AND SLOPED STEEPLY INTO THE MAIN STREET.

IT WOULD HAVE REQUIRED AN EXPERIENCED MAN TO KEEP THE TOP-HEAVY SLED UPRIGHT.

HAL WAS NOT SUCH A MAN.

THE DOGS WERE ANGRY BECAUSE OF THE ILL TREATMENT AND THE UNJUST LOAD.

BUCK WAS RAGING. HE BROKE INTO A RUN AND THE TEAM FOLLOWED HIS LEAD.

KIND-HEARTED CITIZENS CAUGHT THE DOGS AND GATHERED UP THE SCATTERED REMAINS. ALSO, THEY GAVE ADVICE.

"HALF THE LOAD AND TWICE THE DOGS, IF YOU EVER EXPECT TO REACH DAWSON."

"ENOUGH BLANKETS FOR A HOTEL. HALF AS MANY IS TOO MUCH."

"THROW AWAY THAT TENT AND ALL THOSE DISHES."

"GOOD LORD, DO YOU THINK YOU'RE TRAVELLING ON A PULLMAN ?"

AND SO IT WENT, THE INEXORABLE ELIMINA-TION OF THE SUPER-FLUOUS.

MERCEDES CRIED.

SHE CRIED IN GENERAL, AND SHE CRIED IN PARTICULAR OVER EACH DISCARDED THING.

CHARLES AND HAL WENT OUT THAT EVENING AND BOUGHT SIX OUTSIDE DOGS. THESE BROUGHT THE TEAM UP TO FOURTEEN.

IN THE NATURE OF ARCTIC TRAVEL THERE WAS A REASON WHY FOURTEEN DOGS SHOULD NOT DRAG ONE SLED. AND THAT WAS THAT ONE SLED COULD NOT CARRY THE FOOD FOR FOURTEEN DOGS.

BUT CHARLES AND HAL DID NOT KNOW THIS.

IT WAS INEVITABLE THAT THEY SHOULD GO SHORT ON DOG FOOD.

BUT THEY HASTENED IT BY OVERFEEDING, BRINGING THE DAY NEARER WHEN UNDER-FEEDING WOULD COMMENCE.

THEY CUT DOWN EVEN THE ORTHODOX RATION AND TRIED TO INCREASE THE DAY'S TRAVEL.

THEIR OWN INABILITY TO GET UNDER-WAY EARLIER IN THE MORNING PRE-VENTED THEM FROM TRAVELLING LONGER HOURS.

NOT ONLY DID THEY NOT KNOW HOW TO WORK DOGS, BUT THEY DID NOT KNOW HOW TO WORK THEMSELVES.

IT WAS A SIMPLE MATTER TO GIVE THE DOGS LESS FOOD; BUT IT WAS IMPOS-SIBLE TO MAKE THE DOGS TRAVEL FASTER.

IT IS A SAYING OF THE COUNTRY THAT AN OUTSIDE DOG STARVES TO DEATH ON THE RATION OF A HUSKY.

SO THE SIX OUTSIDE DOGS UNDER BUCK COULD DO NO LESS THAN DIE ON HALF THE RATION OF A HUSKY.

BY THIS TIME ALL THE AMENITIES AND GENTLENESSES OF THE SOUTHLAND HAD FALLEN AWAY FROM THE THREE PEOPLE.

SHORN OF ITS GLAMOUR AND ROMANCE, ARCTIC TRAVEL BECAME TO THEM A REALITY TOO HARSH FOR THEIR MANHOOD AND WOMANHOOD.

TO QUARREL WAS THE ONLY THING THEY WERE NEVER TOO WEARY TO DO.

AND THROUGH IT ALL BUCK STAGGERED ALONG AT THE HEAD OF THE TEAM AS IN A NIGHTMARE.

IT WAS HEARTBREAKING, ONLY BUCK'S HEART WAS UNBREAKABLE. THE MAN IN THE RED SWEATER HAD PROVED THAT.

HE PULLED WHEN HE COULD; WHEN HE COULD NO LONGER PULL HE FELL DOWN AND REMAINED DOWN TILL BLOWS FROM WHIP OR CLUB DROVE HIM TO HIS FEET AGAIN.

THE GHOSTLY WINTER SILENCE HAD GIVEN WAY TO THE GREAT SPRING MURMUR OF AWAKENING LIFE.

THE YUKON WAS STRAINING TO BREAK LOOSE THE ICE THAT BOUND IT DOWN.

IT ATE FROM BENEATH; THE SUN ATE FROM ABOVE.

BUCK AND THORNTON HEARD MERCEDES SCREAM, THEN SAW DOGS AND HUMANS DISAPPEAR. THE BOTTOM HAD DROPPED OUT OF THE TRAIL.

YOU POOR DEVIL.

WHEN JOHN THORNTON FROZE HIS FEET THE PREVIOUS DECEMBER, HIS PARTNERS HAD MADE HIM COMFORTABLE AND LEFT HIM TO GET WELL.

AND HERE, BUCK SLOWLY WON BACK HIS STRENGTH.

BUCK WAXED LAZY AS HIS WOUNDS HEALED, HIS MUSCLES SWELLED OUT, AND THE FLESH CAME BACK TO COVER HIS BONES.

THE MAN HAD SAVED HIS LIFE, BUT FURTHER HE WAS THE IDEAL MASTER. HE SAW TO THE WELFARE OF HIS DOGS AS IF THEY WERE HIS OWN CHILDREN, BECAUSE HE COULD NOT HELP IT.

LOVE, GENUINE PASSIONATE LOVE, WAS BUCK'S FOR THE FIRST TIME.

HE WOULD GAZE AT THE MAN BY THE HOUR, HIS HEART SHINING OUT OF HIS EYES.

MONTHS LATER, WHEN THORNTON'S PARTNERS, HANS AND PETE, ARRIVED ON THE LONG-EXPECTED RAFT, BUCK REFUSED TO NOTICE THEM TILL HE LEARNED THEY WERE CLOSE TO THORNTON.

BUT THESE MEN WERE OF THE SAME LARGE TYPE AS THORNTON, AND THEY UNDERSTOOD BUCK AND HIS WAYS.

I'M NOT HANKERING TO BE THE MAN THAT LAYS HANDS ON YOU WHILE HE'S AROUND.

BY JINGO! NOT MINE-SELF EITHER!

IT WAS AT CIRCLE CITY, ERE THE YEAR WAS OUT, THAT PETE'S APPREHENSIONS WERE REALIZED. "BLACK" BURTON, A MAN EVIL-TEMPERED AND MALICIOUS, STRUCK THORNTON.

BUCK'S BODY ROSE UP IN THE AIR AS HE LEFT THE FLOOR FOR THE MAN'S THROAT.

THE MAN SUCCEEDED ONLY IN PARTLY BLOCKING, AND HIS THROAT WAS TORN OPEN.

BUCK'S REPUTATION WAS MADE, AND FROM THAT DAY HIS NAME SPREAD THROUGH EVERY CAMP IN ALASKA.

LATER ON, IN THE FALL OF THE YEAR, BUCK SAVED JOHN THORNTON'S LIFE IN QUITE ANOTHER FASHION.

THEY WERE LINING A POLING BOAT DOWN A BAD STRETCH OF RAPIDS ON THE FORTY MILE CREEK...

...WHEN HANS CHECKED THE BOAT TOO SUDDENLY.

THEY ATTACHED THE LINE WITH WHICH THEY HAD BEEN SNUBBING THE BOAT TO BUCK'S NECK AND SHOULDERS.

BUCK SPRANG IN ON THE INSTANT.

STRANGLING, SUFFOCATING, DRAGGING OVER THE JAGGED BOTTOM, SMASHING AGAINST ROCKS AND SNAGS, THEY VEERED IN TO THE BANK.

IT WAS BROUGHT ABOUT BY A CONVERSATION IN THE ELDORADO SALOON.

MY DOG CAN START A SLED WITH FIVE HUNDRED POUNDS AND WALK OFF WITH IT.

HA! SIX HUNDRED FOR MY DOG!

BUCK CAN START A *THOUSAND* POUNDS.

AND WALK IT A HUNDRED YARDS.

AND BREAK IT OUT? AND WALK OFF WITH IT FOR A HUNDRED YARDS?

WELL, I'VE GOT A THOUSAND DOLLARS SAYS HE CAN'T.

AND THERE IT IS.

NOBODY SPOKE. THORNTON'S BLUFF, IF BLUFF IT WAS, HAD BEEN CALLED.

THORNTON'S TONGUE HAD TRICKED HIM.

HALF A TON!

FURTHER, HE HAD NO THOUSAND DOLLARS; NOR HAD HANS OR PETE.

I'VE GOT A SLED OUTSIDE WITH TWENTY FIFTY-POUND SACKS OF FLOUR ON IT. DON'T LET *THAT* HINDER YOU.

BUCK...
DAMN YOU,
BUCK...

GAD, SIR! GAD!
I'LL GIVE YOU A
THOUSAND FOR HIM,
SIR, A THOUSAND,
SIR-- TWELVE HUN-
DRED, SIR.

...NO, SIR.
YOU CAN GO TO
HELL, SIR. IT'S THE
BEST I CAN DO
FOR YOU, SIR.

WHEN BUCK EARNED SIXTEEN HUN-
DRED DOLLARS IN FIVE MINUTES
FOR JOHN THORNTON, HE MADE IT
POSSIBLE FOR HIS MASTER TO JOURNEY
WITH HIS PARTNERS INTO THE EAST AFTER
A FABLED LOST MINE.

THE LOST
CABIN MINE.

EACH DAY THEY WORKED EARNED
THEM THOUSANDS OF DOLLARS
IN CLEAN DUST AND NUGGETS,
AND THEY WORKED EVERY DAY.

FOR WEEKS AT A TIME THEY
WOULD HOLD ON STEADILY;
AND FOR WEEKS UPON END
THEY WOULD CAMP.

SPRING CAME ON ONCE
MORE, AND AT THE END
OF THEIR WANDERING
THEY FOUND NOT THE
LOST CABIN, BUT A
SHALLOW PLACE WHERE
THE GOLD SHOWED
LIKE BUTTER.

THEY
SOUGHT
NO
FARTHER.

THERE WAS NOTHING FOR THE
DOGS TO DO, AND BUCK SPENT
LONG HOURS MUSING BY THE
FIRE.

THE CALL SOUNDED FROM
THE DEPTHS OF THE FOREST,
FILLING HIM WITH A GREAT
UNREST AND STRANGE DESIRES.

HE SAT BY JOHN THORNTON'S FIRE, BUT BEHIND HIM WERE THE SHADES OF ALL MANNER OF DOGS, HALF-WOLVES, AND WILD WOLVES.

AS OFTEN AS HE HEARD THIS CALL, MYSTERIOUSLY THRILLING AND LURING, HE FELT COMPELLED TO PLUNGE INTO THE FOREST.

BUT AS OFTEN AS HE GAINED THE UNBROKEN EARTH AND GREEN SHADE, THE LOVE OF JOHN THORNTON DREW HIM BACK.

IRRESISTABLE IMPULSES SEIZED HIM. ONE NIGHT HE SPRANG THROUGH THE SLEEPING CAMP AND IN SWIFT SILENCE DASHED THROUGH THE WOODS.

FROM THE FOREST CAME THE CALL, DISTINCT AND DEFINITE AS NEVER BEFORE.

BUCK REMEMBERED JOHN THORNTON.

FOR TWO DAYS AND NIGHTS BUCK NEVER LEFT CAMP, NEVER LET THORNTON OUT OF HIS SIGHT.

BUT AFTER TWO DAYS THE CALL BEGAN TO SOUND MORE IMPERIOUSLY THAN EVER.

HE WANDERED FOR A WEEK, SEEKING VAINLY FOR SIGN OF THE WILD BROTHER.

THE BLOOD-LONGING BECAME STRONGER THAN EVER BEFORE. HE WAS A KILLER, A THING THAT PREYED ON LIVING THINGS.

HE KILLED TO EAT, NOT FROM WANTONESS; BUT HE PREFERRED TO EAT WHAT HE KILLED HIMSELF.

As the fall of the year came on, the moose appeared in greater abundance, moving slowly down to meet the winter in the lower valleys.

Chief among the moose was a great bull.

He was in a savage temper, and as formidable an antagonist as ever Buck could desire.

Buck proceeded to cut the bull from the herd.

It was no slight task. The bull charged Buck, who retreated craftily.

There is a patience of the wild--dogged, tireless, persistent as life itself.

At last, at the end of the fourth day...

Night and day, Buck never left his prey, never gave it a moment's rest. Never permitted it to browse the leaves of trees, or to slake its burning thirst.

FOR A DAY AND NIGHT HE REMAINED BY THE KILL, EATING AND SLEEPING, TURN AND TURN ABOUT. THEN, RESTED, FRESH AND STRONG, HE TURNED HIS FACE TOWARD CAMP AND JOHN THORNTON.

AS HE LOPED ON HE BECAME MORE AND MORE CONSCIOUS OF A NEW STIR IN THE LAND.

HE CAME UPON A FRESH TRAIL THAT SENT HIS NECK HAIR RIPPLING AND BRISTLING.

IT LED STRAIGHT TOWARD CAMP AND JOHN THORNTON.

FROM THE CAMP CAME THE FAINT SOUND OF MANY VOICES, RISING AND FALLING IN A SINGSONG CHANT.

BELLYING FORWARD TO THE EDGE OF THE CLEARING, HE FOUND HANS, LYING ON HIS FACE, FEATHERED WITH ARROWS.

THE YEEHATS WERE DANCING WHEN THEY HEARD A FEARFUL ROARING AND SAW RUSHING UPON THEM AN ANIMAL THE LIKE OF WHICH THEY HAD NEVER SEEN BEFORE.

BUCK WAS THE FIEND INCARNATE, RAGING AT THEIR HEELS AND DRAGGING THEM DOWN LIKE DEER.

BUCK SPRANG UPON THE CHIEF, RIPPING HIS THROAT WIDE OPEN TILL THE RENT JUGULAR SPOUTED A FOUNTAIN OF BLOOD.

THEY HAD DIED SO EASILY.

THEY WERE NO MATCH AT ALL, WERE IT NOT FOR THEIR ARROWS AND SPEARS... AND CLUBS.

BUCK SCENTED EVERY DETAIL OF THORNTON'S DESPERATE STRUGGLE.

FOR BUCK FOLLOWED HIS TRACE INTO THE WATER, FROM WHICH NO TRACE LED AWAY.

THE POOL HID WHAT IT CONTAINED, AND IT CONTAINED JOHN THORNTON.

IT LEFT A GREAT VOID IN HIM, SOMEWHAT AKIN TO HUNGER, BUT A VOID WHICH ACHED AND ACHED.

WITH THE COMING OF NIGHT, BUCK BECAME ALIVE TO A STIRRING OF NEW LIFE IN THE FOREST.

INTO THE CLEARING THEY POURED IN A SILVERY FLOOD...

...AND IN THE CENTER OF THE CLEARING STOOD BUCK, WAITING THEIR COMING.

JOHN THORNTON WAS DEAD. THE LAST TIE WAS BROKEN. MAN AND THE CLAIMS OF MAN NO LONGER BOUND HIM.

THE OLD WOLF SAT DOWN, POINTED HIS NOSE AT THE MOON, AND BROKE OUT THE LONG WOLF HOWL.

AND NOW THE CALL CAME TO BUCK IN UNMISTAKABLE ACCENTS.

HE TOO, SAT DOWN AND HOWLED.

THE LEADERS LIFTED THE YELP OF THE PACK AND SWUNG INTO THE WOODS. THE WOLVES SWUNG IN BEHIND, YELPING IN CHORUS. AND BUCK RAN WITH THEM.

AND HERE MAY WELL END THE STORY OF BUCK...

THE YEARS WERE NOT MANY WHEN THE YEEHATS NOTED A CHANGE IN THE BREED OF TIMBER WOLVES; FOR SOME WERE SEEN WITH SPLASHES OF BROWN ON HEAD AND MUZZLE, AND WITH A RIFT OF WHITE CENTERING DOWN THE CHEST.

THEY TELL OF A GHOST DOG THAT HAS GREAT CUNNING, STEALING FROM THEIR CAMPS, ROBBING THEIR TRAPS, SLAYING THEIR DOGS, AND DEFYING THEIR BRAVEST HUNTERS.

AND THERE IS A CERTAIN VALLEY WHICH THE YEEHATS NEVER ENTER. IN THE SUMMER, HOWEVER, THERE IS ONE VISITOR.

HE CROSSES ALONE FROM THE TIMBER LAND AND COMES DOWN TO AN OPEN SPACE AMONG THE TREES. HERE A YELLOW STREAM FLOWS FROM ROTTING MOOSEHIDE SACKS AND SINKS INTO THE GROUND.

HERE HE MUSES FOR A TIME..,

..HOWLING ONCE, LONG AND MOURN-FULLY..,

..,HIS GREAT THROAT A-BELLOW AS HE SINGS THE SONG OF A YOUNGER WORLD..,

..,WHICH IS THE SONG OF THE PACK.

JACK LONDON was born in San Francisco on January 12, 1876. He was raised in poverty along the Oakland waterfront; to help support his family, London sold newspapers and performed odd jobs. At the age of 14, London quit school and went to work full time in a cannery. His love of boys' adventure fiction influenced him to turn pirate at the age of 16, when he used his sloop *Razzle Dazzle* to raid the oyster beds in San Francisco Bay. In an example of the contradictions which were later to inform his fiction, the next year found him working alongside the harbor police to stop such piracy. After spending a year at sea on a sealing expedition and traveling the country as a tramp, London finished high school and briefly attended the University of California. In 1897, he joined the Klondike gold rush. Although success in the gold fields eluded him, the experience gave him valuable insight into the rugged individualists who populated the raw frontier. London returned to Oakland and took up writing; he sold his first short story, "To the Man on the Trail," to the *Overland Monthly* in 1898. By 1900, he had published enough of his tales of the Yukon to warrant a collection, *The Son of the Wolf*. London's stories of the vigorous and often brutal life in the far north found a ready audience, and his style — raw, excitable, but always readable — was successful among both young and old. His fame was assured when *The Call of the Wild* was published to great acclamation in 1903. A passionate believer in socialism and a champion of the working class — views advocated in such novels as *The Iron Heel* (1908) and *The Valley of the Moon* (1913) — London nevertheless also subscribed to Nietzche's cult of "red blood." Much of London's fiction, including *The Sea Wolf* (1904) and *The Abysmal Brute* (1913), is populated by characters stripped of social conventions to reveal the inhuman brute that lies beneath the veneer of civilization. The Darwinian concept of survival of the fittest is also a recurrent theme in his fiction. London published 51 books — all well received — during his 17-year writing career, but his later works never achieved the popularity of *The Call of the Wild*. Frustrated by what he perceived as his failure, and plagued by bouts of alcoholism and rheumatism, London died in 1916 at the age of 40. In a eulogy, his daughter, Joan, described London — along with Stephen Crane and Frank Norris — as "the three young pioneers who at the turn of the century had blazed the literary trails into modern American literature."

RICARDO VILLAGRAN was born in Buenos Aires, Argentina in 1938. As a youth, he studied and emulated the works of great American comics artists like Hal Foster (*Prince Valiant*) and Alex Raymond (*Flash Gordon*). Villagran worked for years as an assistant to some of South America's greatest comic illustrators. Striking out on his own, he formed an art studio and created some of Europe's and South America's best-known illustrated characters. Villagran's art has been featured in a wide range of popular titles, including *Batman*, *Star Trek*, *Evangeline*, *Atari Force*, and his own graphic novel, *Ka-Zar*. Villagran continues to reside in Argentina.

CHARLES DIXON was born in Philadelphia in 1954. In the comics field, he has written for the fantasy favorite, *Conan the Barbarian,* and has contributed to *Airboy*, *Moon Knight*, *Winter World*, and *Alien Legion* . The co-creator of *Evangeline*, Dixon also has written several *Raggedy Ann* and *Winnie the Pooh* children's books.

WATCH FOR THESE OTHER GREAT

CLASSIC READING

CLASSIC ENTERTAINMENT

CLASSICS ILLUSTRATED.®

The Raven and Other Poems • Great Expectations • Through the Looking-Glass • Moby Dick • Hamlet • The Scarlet Letter • The Count of Monte Cristo • Dr. Jekyll and Mr. Hyde • The Adventures of Tom Sawyer • The Call of the Wild • Rip Van Winkle • The Island of Dr. Moreau • Wuthering Heights • The Fall of the House of Usher • The Gift of the Magi and Other Stories • A Christmas Carol • Treasure Island • The Devil's Dictionary • The Secret Agent • Faust • Ivanhoe • The Jungle • Cyrano de Bergerac • The Invisible Man • Robinson Crusoe • Aesop's Fables • The Red Badge of Courage • The Hunchback of Notre Dame • Around the World in 80 Days • Heart of Darkness • The Adventures of Huckleberry Finn • All Quiet on the Western Front • Paradise Lost • The Last of the Mohicans • Candide • Arabian Nights • Frankenstein • The Three Musketeers • Alice in Wonderland • The Lost World • Don Quixote